AF616035

Photo by Gerry Goodstein

Pamela Reed in a scene from the Manhattan Theatre Club production of "Standing On My Knees." Setting by David Emmons.

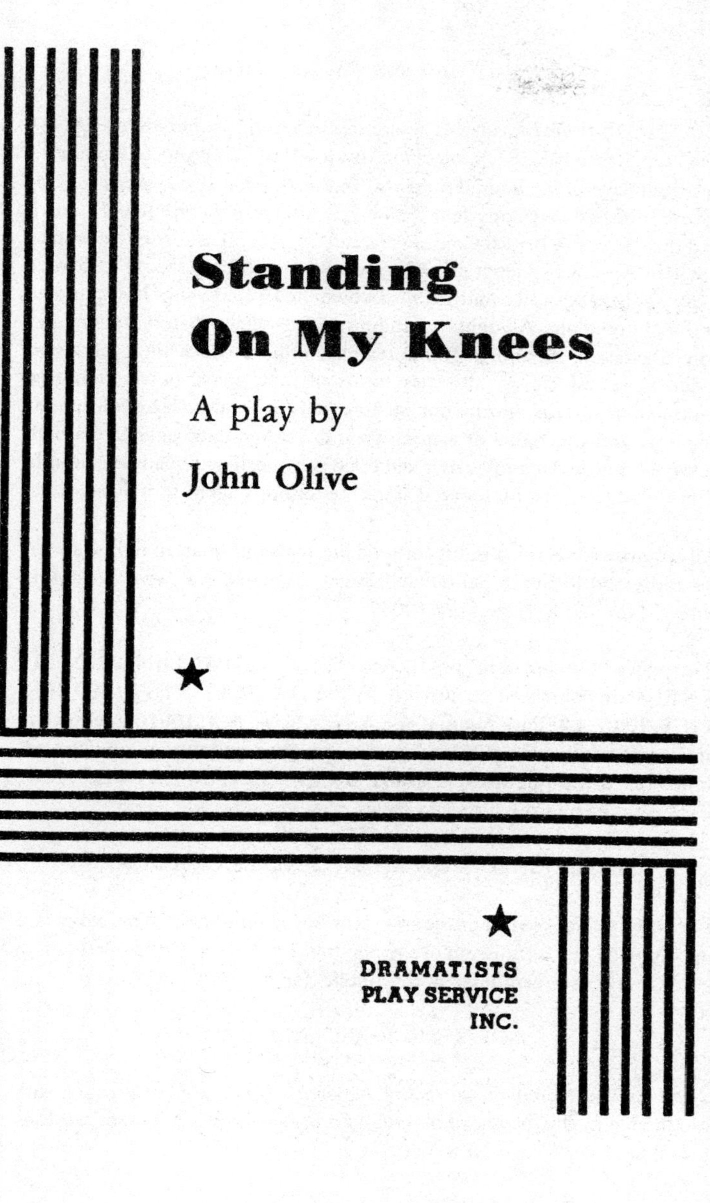

Standing On My Knees

A play by

John Olive

DRAMATISTS
PLAY SERVICE
INC.

SPECIAL NOTE ON MUSIC AND RECORDINGS

For performance of such music and recordings mentioned in this play as are in copyright, the permission of the copyright owners must be obtained, or other music and recordings in the public domain substituted.

SOUND EFFECTS RECORD

The following sound effects record, which may be used in connection with production of this play, can be obtained from Thomas J. Valentino, Inc., 151 West 46th Street, New York, N.Y. 10036.

No. 5025 — Telephone ring

STANDING ON MY KNEES was first produced professionally in Chicago at Wisdom Bridge Theatre, Robert Falls, Artistic Director, Jeffrey Ortmann, Executive Director. The production was directed by Robert Falls; the set was by John Murbach; costumes were by Douglas J. Koertge; lighting was by Gary Heitz; and the production was stage managed by Susan Hope.

CAST

CATHERINE . . . . Kit Flanagan
ROBERT . . . . Robert Neches
JOANNE . . . . Susan Dafoe
ALICE . . . . Jodean Culbert

The play opened in December, 1981

STANDING ON MY KNEES was produced in New York at the Manhattan Theatre Club, Lynne Meadow, Artistic Director, Barry Grove, Managing Director. The production was directed by Robert Falls; the set was by David Emmons; costumes were by Nan Cibula; lighting was by William Mintzer; and the production was stage managed by Johnna Murray.

CAST

CATHERINE . . . . Pamela Reed
ROBERT . . . . Robert Neches

JOANNE . . . . Tresa Hughes
ALICE . . . . Jean De Baer

The play opened in October, 1982

Place: a large American city

Time: the present, during the winter

This play is dedicated to the memory of
Elizabeth Brinkman Olive.

THE SETTING

The stage is divided into two areas. Catherine's small cluttered apartment occupies the most prominent part. It contains: a kitchen table, a small writing desk, a surprisingly expensive stereo system, a small bed, a few chairs and lots of books and records. The rest of the stage is bare. Individual set pieces are placed on this bare stage as needed. Joanne's area, located as far as possible from Catherine's apartment, contains a small desk and two chairs.

STANDING ON MY KNEES

ACT ONE

As the audience enters the theatre, Catherine is already onstage, sleeping in her small bed. A magazine lies on the bed next to her and her reading light is on; she is bathed in a small pool of warm light. The rest of the apartment is dark. Music is heard playing softly on the stereo: Schoenberg's "Pierrot Lunaire—" soft, dissonant. Finally, the house lights and the lights on the stage fade to Blackout.*

Alice and Joanne enter, and stand on either side of the stage, not lit. Lights fade back up on Catherine; she stirs in her sleep, slightly.

JOANNE. (*In darkness, very soft.*) Catherine.
ALICE. (*Also in darkness, softly.*) Catherine.
JOANNE. Catherine?
ALICE. (*Voice overlapping, blending with Joanne's.*) Cath—
JOANNE. (*Overlapping.*) Cath—
ALICE. —erine?
ALICE and JOANNE. Catherine?
JOANNE. (*A bit louder.*) Can you hear me? (*Pause. Catherine stirs again.*) Just nod your head if you can.

*See Special Note on copyright page.

ALICE. Catherine.
JOANNE. Do the voices come more often at night? (*Slight pause.*) Do you recognize them? Are they always in an understandable language? (*Slight pause.*) Catherine, how often do you feel there are other people inside your body? Do they touch you? Caress you? Strike you? Hurt you?
ALICE. I can't come visit you anymore.
JOANNE. Do the voices tell you what to do?
ALICE. I just can't walk down those godawful, puke green hospital corridors anymore.
JOANNE. Do they shout?
ALICE. (*Overlapping again, building.*) I don't think you want me to anyway.
JOANNE. Mock you? Whisper to you? Argue with you?
ALICE. It's like taking a shortcut to the future of the world, and I can't do that—
JOANNE. Argue with you? Argue? Argue?
ALICE. —I have to make a living.
ALICE and JOANNE. (*A crescendo.*) Catherine? Catherine! (*Catherine, startled, sits up abruptly.*)
CATHERINE. What!? What? Alice! (*Slight pause.*) Alice? (*Slight pause.*) What? (*Catherine sits for a long moment, rubbing her eyes, calming herself.*) Wow. (*Stands, goes to the stereo, rejects the record. Goes to the kitchen, gets a glass of water, drinks it. Glances at a clock, notices the time, grabs the clock, checking to see if it's working.*) Oh shit. (*Joanne enters the bare stage area. Catherine grabs her coat, goes quickly to the bare stage area, meets Joanne.*)
JOANNE. Catherine?
CATHERINE. Hi.
JOANNE. Hello.
CATHERINE. Am I late?
JOANNE. No, not at all. This way, please. Have a seat. (*They go to Joanne's area and sit: Joanne at her desk, Catherine at a chair. Slight pause.*) Good to see you.
CATHERINE. Thanks.

JOANNE. You're looking well.
CATHERINE. Thanks.
JOANNE. Well. This is my office. We'll be meeting here from now on.
CATHERINE. Nice.
JOANNE. Yes, it is. Much nicer than those dreary conference rooms at the hospital.
CATHERINE. That a picture of your husband?
JOANNE. My father.
CATHERINE. (*Laughs.*) Oh. Open mouth, insert foot.
JOANNE. Did you take the bus down today?
CATHERINE. (*After a short pause.*) Yes.
JOANNE. How've you been feeling?
CATHERINE. Okay.
JOANNE. Settled into your apartment?
CATHERINE. I cleaned. All weekend. Very strange behavior for me. And I went shopping. Groceries. Four new record albums I couldn't afford. And I called my parents.
JOANNE. Yes?
CATHERINE. Everything feels . . . all right. I guess.
JOANNE. Any symptoms?
CATHERINE. (*After a pause.*) I don't think so.
JOANNE. (*Looks at her, then starts to write in her notes.*) Good.
CATHERINE. And . . . I went to a party.
JOANNE. Really. (*Music: Coltrane's "Traneing In."**) Did you have a good time?
CATHERINE. No. (*Catherine stands, moves away from Joanne. Robert enters.*)
ROBERT. (*Jovially.*) Hi.
CATHERINE. Hello.
ROBERT. (*Smiles as he passes her.*) Excuse me.
CATHERINE. Occupied.
ROBERT. Hm?

*See Special Note on copyright page.

CATHERINE. It's occupied.
ROBERT. Oh. That's too bad. Well, I'll . . . (*Starts to exit.*) See you later?
CATHERINE. Sure. (*Robert exits.*) But I'm glad I went. I wanted to see Alice.
JOANNE. We need our friends.
CATHERINE. There were too many people there. Too many . . . voices. (*Short pause, then Joanne starts to write in her notes.*) Why are you writing that down?
ALICE. (*From offstage.*) There you are. (*Enters.*) I been lookin' for you, what you doin' out here?
CATHERINE. (*Gestures toward an imaginary bookshelf.*) Book titles.
ALICE. You okay?
CATHERINE. (*Patiently—she hates the question.*) I'm fine. It's a nice party. I just. . . .
ALICE. Yeah.
CATHERINE. Wine's tastin' good.
ALICE. Oh, right, the wine. Ed bought it. He was so proud of himself 'cause it only cost three fifty a gallon. We're all gonna have thundering headaches in the morning.
CATHERINE. (*Laughs.*) It's good. Seems like all I've had to drink the past few months been orange juice. (*Beat.*) It's good to see you, Alice.
ALICE. Yeah?
CATHERINE. Yeah. I appreciate the invitation.
ALICE. Bill says hi. He's at a conference out east so he couldn't make it. Sarah says hi. She's pregnant.
CATHERINE. Really? Oh, that's fantastic. God, how long've I been gone?
ALICE. They say you should stop by the office and maybe I'll let 'em stop working for two minutes so they can look at you, make sure you're real.
CATHERINE. You're all heart.
ALICE. Management techniques. They all love my ass. (*Beat.*) You were gone a long time, babe.

CATHERINE. Yeah.
ALICE. You really all right?
CATHERINE. Alice . . . (*Robert enters.*)
ROBERT. Hi. The bathroom still . . . ?
ALICE. Robert. Meet Catherine. Catherine, meet Robert.
ROBERT. (*Shaking Catherine's shoulder.*) Hi, Catherine.
ALICE. (*Puts her arm around Catherine's shoulder.*) Catherine is our best poet. That's because she's my discovery. She's much too young to be as good as she is. Robert is Ed's discovery.
ROBERT. I'm not a poet, I assure you.
ALICE. Robert brokes stocks.
ROBERT. "Investment consultation," as my colleagues say. A fancy name for a dull, very profitable job.
ALICE. (*After a pause.*) Well, I'll leave you two lovebirds alone. (*Kisses Catherine's forehead.*) I'm glad you're here. (*Exits.*)
ROBERT. Can I get you some more wine?
CATHERINE. No, thanks.
ROBERT. It's awful, isn't it? Nothing worse than bad rose.
CATHERINE. Or good rose.
ROBERT. Ed's desperate to get rid of it.
CATHERINE. He can put it in his motorcycle.
ROBERT. Alice made him sell it. Didn't you hear about that?
CATHERINE. No, I. . . .
ROBERT. Poor Ed. But she was right, he's getting too old for that sort of thing. (*Slight pause.*) Am I following you?
CATHERINE. Are you?
ROBERT. (*Gestures toward the bathroom.*) No, I meant. . . .
CATHERINE. (*Gestures towards the books.*) No, I'm just. . . .
ROBERT. Alice has a fantastic library.
CATHERINE. Scary thing is she's read 'em all.
ROBERT. Really?

CATHERINE. Yeah.

ROBERT. Incredible. (*Pauses again.*) Wanna come in, join the party?

CATHERINE. Well, no, I'm . . . maybe later.

ROBERT. It's pretty rancid in there.

CATHERINE. There's another one upstairs.

ROBERT. Hm? Oh, yeah, I better. . . . (*Starts to exit, turns.*) Um . . .

CATHERINE. Hm?

ROBERT. Nothing. Nice to meet you, Catherine.

CATHERINE. Yeah, me too. (*Robert exits. Light on Joanne intensifies.*)

JOANNE. How can I put this? Sometimes, the intensity of your need for something makes that something impossible to get. You need friends desperately but you can't make contact because you're afraid that people will sense your desperation. And maybe they do. Maybe that makes you and them turn away. The more you need, the less you get.

CATHERINE. I think I'll have that sewn into a sampler. (*Puts on her coat, gets ready to leave. Robert enters.*)

ROBERT. Say—Oh, leaving?

CATHERINE. Yes.

ROBERT. Well, listen . . .

CATHERINE. Hm?

ROBERT. Could I possibly get your phone number?

CATHERINE. 556-1093

ROBERT. Wait a minute, hold it. (*Fumbles in his pockets, gets out pen and paper.*) Once again?

CATHERINE. 5-5-6. 1-0-9-3.

ROBERT. Thanks. See you. (*Robert exits. Alice enters.*)

JOANNE. Catherine?

ALICE. Catherine.

ALICE and JOANNE. Catherine.

CATHERINE. Yes.

JOANNE. You seem nervous.

CATHERINE. Well, yeah.

JOANNE. Sleeping all right?
CATHERINE. (*Shrugs.*) I dunno.
JOANNE. Dreams?
CATHERINE. (*Slight pause.*) Yeah.
JOANNE. (*Looks at her notes.*) Let's try the Thorazine at . . . two hundred milligrams at bedtime.
CATHERINE. That's probably a good idea. Other dosages the same?
JOANNE. For now.
ALICE. (*Steps forward.*) Catherine.
CATHERINE. Alice, I had a great time, I really did, really super party. Just past my bedtime, y'know?
ALICE. (*Gives Catherine a quick hug.*) I'm happy you came. Can we have lunch? Monday?
CATHERINE. Yeah, sure.
ALICE. I'll have to look in my book, but I think Monday's okay.
CATHERINE. Okay.
ALICE. (*Steps into the shadows.*) Good. I'm glad you came. (*Alice exits. Catherine steps into her apartment, sits on the bed.*)
CATHERINE. Joanne, I still don't think I was ready to be released.
JOANNE. I know.
CATHERINE. It's hard to make contact with anything. My apartment, my books, my friends. I'm afraid it's all going to . . . melt. (*Pauses.*) I don't believe it's winter. I lost, completely lost, three months.
JOANNE. Are you really so surprised?
CATHERINE. I dunno. It's always been there, I've even been hospitalized before. But this time, I just wasn't. . . . I don't know.
JOANNE. Do you blame yourself for the illness?
CATHERINE. I just don't want it to come back. Do you think it'll come back?
JOANNE. (*After a pause.*) I don't know, Catherine. But if

it does, this time, you have me, you have your friends. We just have to take it day by day. It's going to be hard, but I have confidence in you. (*Joanne's light starts to fade.*) I'll see you Friday. (*Joanne's light disappears. A pause, then Catherine rises, puts on a record. Music: John Cage's "Concerto for Prepared Piano."* Catherine then takes out a tray filled with medicine bottles—mostly vitamins but there is one very large prescription bottle—then gets a glass of water and starts eating pills.*)

CATHERINE. Vitamins for the imbalance. Aspirin for the headache. Thorazine for the dreams and the blood. Thorazine to coagulate the blood. (*Lays down on the small bed.*) Now I lay me down to snore. And pray the dreams will come no more. If I'm lucky, up by ten. And then I'll lay me down again. A poet. (*Lights fade on the apartment. A spot fades up on Robert in the bare stage area. Phone starts to ring. Note: the convention, established here, is that the characters speaking to Catherine on the phone simply focus out over the audience, whereas Catherine uses an actual phone. Lights up on the apartment. Catherine groans, gets up, goes to the phone and answers it, just as Robert shrugs and starts to move out of his light.*) Hello.

ROBERT. (*Steps back into his light.*) Hello?

CATHERINE. Hello?

ROBERT. Hi.

CATHERINE. Hello?

ROBERT. Catherine?

CATHERINE. Yes.

ROBERT. Hello, it's Robert.

CATHERINE. Who?

ROBERT. Robert.

CATHERINE. Robert?

ROBERT. From the party this weekend. Alice's party. You don't remember me and I woke you up. Great.

*See Special Note on copyright page.

CATHERINE. What time is it?
ROBERT. (*Looks at his watch.*) Almost eleven. I could call back.
CATHERINE. No, I'm up now.
ROBERT. Sorry.
CATHERINE. It's all right. It was a a . . . vague party.
ROBERT. Yes, it certainly was. Vague.
CATHERINE. Did you ever get into the bathroom?
ROBERT. I did, and it was the climax of the evening. (*Pauses.*) Maybe I should call back.
CATHERINE. What do you do, anyway?
ROBERT. (*Hesitates.*) Investment consultation.
CATHERINE. Oh, that's right, you break stocks.
ROBERT. Yes.
CATHERINE. You wearing a three piece suit?
ROBERT. (*Slight pause.*) Yes.
CATHERINE. How many do you own?
ROBERT. Seven, I think.
CATHERINE. One for every—
ROBERT. But my favorite is this thick old wool Scottish smoking jacket. Twigs and clods of dirt are still working their way out of the tweed.
CATHERINE. And during a full moon, it steams. I'm always a smartass when I wake up.
ROBERT. What do you do?
CATHERINE. Do? Well . . .
ROBERT. I mean, I know you're a writer, a poet, but—
CATHERINE. But what do I do for a living?
ROBERT. Do you teach?
CATHERINE. No. God, no.
ROBERT. (*Clears his throat.*) What I'm getting at, stupidly, is: do you maybe have time for lunch, sometime this week?
CATHERINE. (*After a slight pause.*) What would your wife say?
ROBERT. I don't know, I haven't seen her in six years.
CATHERINE. I like Chinese.

ROBERT. Wednesday? Wednesday okay?

CATHERINE. Thursday would be better.

ROBERT. Okay. You know that seaweed green statue in front of the library?

CATHERINE. Noon?

ROBERT. Fine. I'll look forward to it, Catherine.

CATHERINE. So will I, Robert. See you then. (*Hangs up.*)

ROBERT. Bye. (*Exits. A spot fades up on Alice sitting at a table in the bare stage area with the remains of lunch and a bottle of German wine. Catherine starts to get dressed. A pause, then Catherine and Alice both start speaking at once.*)

ALICE. You want some—?

CATHERINE. (*Overlapping.*) How's business?

ALICE. What?

CATHERINE. Hm?

ALICE. (*Laughing.*) You want some more wine?

CATHERINE. No.

ALICE. Coffee?

CATHERINE. Caffeine makes you crazy.

ALICE. Oh. Dessert?

CATHERINE. No.

ALICE. This is a good place, don't you think? German food.

CATHERINE. How's business?

ALICE. Oh, good. *The Woman's Guide to Baseball's* a big hit. Still understaffed, still have to type my own letters, pain in the ass. God, you look good.

CATHERINE. I feel good. All that healthy hospital food. (*Catherine, dressed, goes to the table and sits.*)

ALICE. (*After a beat.*) So.

CATHERINE. Hm?

ALICE. What was it like?

CATHERINE. (*Pauses, shrugs.*) You saw me.

ALICE. Yeah, Jesus, I'll never forget it.

CATHERINE. I don't remember a lot of it. Time flew.

ALICE. Because of the drugs? Thorazine, right?

CATHERINE. Plus a lot of vitamins. Megavitamins. "Orthomolecular Therapy." But mostly Thorazine.

ALICE. The Thorazine make you feel like your brain's gained fifteen pounds?

CATHERINE. It does slow everything down.

ALICE. Yeah? Can I have some? (*A beat, looks away.*) Okay, okay. (*Another beat.*) The hospital's all right, isn't it? I mean, it's not . . . Cuckoo's Nest, padded isolation chambers, sadistic nurses, a huge institutional toilet?

CATHERINE. No, it's nice. There's a real sense of . . . community.

ALICE. Yeah? The other patients interesting?

CATHERINE. Yeah.

ALICE. You miss 'em?

CATHERINE. Yeah.

ALICE. You glad to be out?

CATHERINE. No.

ALICE. (*After an uncomfortable pause.*) Ed's fine. Some tiny town in Iowa commissioned him to make a huge bronze football for the civic center. He quit bein' a vegetarian, we don't talk much. Wants to go to Mexico. Beer is better there. You're makin' me nervous, babe.

CATHERINE. I make everybody nervous, I know. I feel like I should be wearing a big scarlet S.

ALICE. (*Nervously, too loud.*) SchizoWoman!!

CATHERINE. Alice.

ALICE. (*Looks around sheepishly.*) Shit. (*A beat.*) Well, I'm jealous, you know that. You get to go lock horns with evil psychiatrists, commune with the supernatural. I have to live with Ed.

CATHERINE. (*Laughs.*) God.

ALICE. I know my curiosity is morbid and you hate me for being the gringo I am. (*A pause. Alice continues, not looking at Catherine.*) So how you coming on the book? Working on it? Thinking about it, at least?

CATHERINE. Thinking about it a lot.

ALICE. Well . . .

CATHERINE. But I haven't been working on it, Alice.
ALICE. Well, why not?
CATHERINE. Alice, I've been very ill.
ALICE. (*Laughs nervously.*) Doesn't that help?
CATHERINE. I can't work on the book right now.
ALICE. You wanna write it off? I'd really rather not. That's a lot of expensive staff time down the—
CATHERINE. Take it easy.
ALICE. (*After a pause.*) You'll start working on it now.
CATHERINE. No.
ALICE. Why?
CATHERINE. Alice.
ALICE. Why?
CATHERINE. I was working on the book when I . . . flipped.
ALICE. So? The book made you crazy? (*Laughs.*)
CATHERINE. (*Voice thick, looking away.*) I don't . . .
ALICE. You gonna stop writing? That what you're saying?
CATHERINE. I have to.
ALICE. (*Laughs again.*) You kidding? You'll never— (*Stops, looks at her.*) It's your best book. I don't believe you're gonna—
CATHERINE. Alice. Stop it. Just— (*Suddenly stands up.*)
ALICE. Hey. You okay?
CATHERINE. Gotta go.
ALICE. Oh shit, babe, don't pay any attention to me, I'm fucked up. You're fucked up, Ed's fucked up, everybody I care about's—
CATHERINE. I'm not fucked up. I'm sick. (*Short pause. Then Alice bursts into laughter. Catherine takes money from her pocket, puts it on the table.*) Here. (*Starts to go.*)
ALICE. Catherine. (*Catherine stops.*) It was gonna be your best book. The best one we ever did. It was gonna be beautiful. (*Stands.*) Take care. (*Exits. Catherine stands alone for a moment, in the bare stage area. Robert enters, joins her.*)

ROBERT. What do you mean?
CATHERINE. Oh, now you didn't go and get offended, did you?
ROBERT. My thought patterns are much more eloquent than that music.
CATHERINE. Okay, all right.
ROBERT. Speak for yourself, gorgeous.
CATHERINE. I just meant that twentieth century music approximates the rhythms of thought more realistically than, say, Bach or the Beatles. I didn't mean that you, personally—
ROBERT. Okay.
CATHERINE. You had a miserable time.
ROBERT. No, not at all. I'm glad you invited me. You cold? Your skin's all ruddy.
CATHERINE. Ruddy?
ROBERT. Well, flushed. You have nice eyes.
CATHERINE. Thanks.
ROBERT. (*Reaches out, touches her face.*) You are cold.
CATHERINE. Little bit.
ROBERT. Why aren't we walking?
CATHERINE. We're here.
ROBERT. (*Looks up at the "building."*) Oh. You live here?
CATHERINE. Yeah?
ROBERT. Okay . . . (*Exuent. From offstage, we hear:*) My favorite part was when they scraped the chair across the stage.
CATHERINE. You liked that, eh?
ROBERT. It brought tears to my eyes. And set my teeth on edge. (*Catherine and Robert enter the apartment.*)
CATHERINE. My humble abode.
ROBERT. Yes.
CATHERINE. You like it?
ROBERT. Like? Well, it's you, very you. And I like you. You wanna take my coat? Here. (*Gives his coat to Catherine; she tosses it on the bed.*) So this is a poet's garret.
CATHERINE. Brown water and all the cockroaches I can eat. I've got a view of the Eiffel Tower scotchtaped to the bath-

room window.

ROBERT. I've never been in one before.

CATHERINE. A bathroom?

ROBERT. A garret.

CATHERINE. Well, as a conservative upper middle class businessman you must be extremely uncomfortable.

ROBERT. Oh, no. I—

CATHERINE. I like where I live.

ROBERT. So do I. I didn't mean—

CATHERINE. I know.

ROBERT. (*Holds up a wine bottle.*) Got a corkscrew?

CATHERINE. I'll get it. Sit. (*Goes to kitchen.*)

ROBERT. Where?

CATHERINE. Just knock those books on the floor.

ROBERT. Okay . . . (*Gingerly pushes a pile of books onto the floor, sits. Catherine gives him a corkscrew.*)

CATHERINE. Here.

ROBERT. Ah. (*Deftly opens the wine.*) Um . . . glasses?

CATHERINE. Are dirty. And redundant.

ROBERT. Redundant?

CATHERINE. Well, I mean the point is to get the wine from the bottle into your belly. There's no reason to temporarily store it in a glass, right?

ROBERT. Right: and given the neighborhood, glasses would be bad form. Skol. (*Takes a swig and immediately spills wine down his chin.*) Shit.

CATHERINE. (*Takes the bottle.*) You'll never make it as a wino, Robert. Lookin' at ya. (*Takes a swig.*) Mm. Has a nice bouncy robustness.

ROBERT. A bit surly.

CATHERINE. Pleasingly impudent, I would say.

ROBERT. Very sort of circular.

CATHERINE. Tastes good, too.

ROBERT. Wanna know what I did?

CATHERINE. Hm?

ROBERT. I went to a bookstore, looking for some of your work.
CATHERINE. Oh.
ROBERT. They'd never heard of you.
CATHERINE. Don't tell me which store. (*Slight pause.*) Downtown?
ROBERT. Yeah. Anyway, what I was wondering—
CATHERINE. Alright. (*Goes to her desk, gets out two slim hardcover books, gives them to Robert.*) This is the first one. It's okay. This is the second one, the one I like.
ROBERT. *Lines.*
CATHERINE. Well, the title . . .
ROBERT. I'll give them back as soon as I—
CATHERINE. You can have them.
ROBERT. Thank you. (*Glances quickly through one, then puts them both aside, carefully.*) Thank you very much. (*They laugh.*)
CATHERINE. Stop Bogarting the bottle.
ROBERT. What? Oh. (*Gives her the bottle.*)
CATHERINE. What. (*Robert looks at her, inquisitively.*) The smile.
ROBERT. You mean the shiteating grin?
CATHERINE. (*Laughs.*) Yeah.
ROBERT. Happens whenever I'm feeling vaguely guilty about having a good time. It'll pass.
CATHERINE. How's business? Maybe it'll help to talk about that.
ROBERT. Business is okay.
CATHERINE. Yeah? (*Laughs.*) Jesus.
ROBERT. I think we're both a little nervous.
CATHERINE. Yeah. Wanna hear some music?
ROBERT. Yeah, something that reflects the rhythms of your thinking.
CATHERINE. Okay, I was bullshitting.
ROBERT. No, no—

CATHERINE. It's all right, I'm glad you called me on it. (*Starts the stereo. Music: Lucas Foss' "Baroque Variations,"* stately, lush, rich.*)

ROBERT. (*Listens for a moment.*) What's this?

CATHERINE. A variation on Handel's Largo. Like it?

ROBERT. Yeah, it's . . . sensuous. (*A pause, then they both laugh, then kiss. The stagelights fade to Blackout. Silence. Then Joanne is heard, as before, speaking in the darkness.*)

JOANNE. Catherine? (*Pause.*) Catherine, can you hear me? (*Pause.*) Do you know where you are, do you know how long you've been here, can you nod your head? (*Pause.*) How often do the voices come? Can you summon them? Control them? And when you feel your body melting, does it affect your vision? (*Pause.*) And the taste of blood? The taste of blood? And the music? Music? Music? (*Pause, a shorter one now.*) This fluid that runs out of your body, can you see it? Only feel it? Taste it? Can other people see it?

CATHERINE. No. . . .

ROBERT. Hm?

JOANNE. Is it blood? Water?

ROBERT. Catherine?

JOANNE. Is it—?

CATHERINE. (*Startled.*) What!? (*Joanne suddenly stops speaking. Lights on the apartment fade up: Catherine and Robert and under the covers of the small bed.*)

ROBERT. How are you doing?

CATHERINE. I dozed.

ROBERT. You dozed? Really? Hard to believe. This bed . . . (*Shifts his weight.*)

CATHERINE. Ow. Move your—

ROBERT. Wait a minute. Can you lift your leg?

CATHERINE. I think so. Aaaggghhh. . . .

ROBERT. There.

CATHERINE. Thanks.

*See Special Note on copyright page.

ROBERT. My arm. Lift your—
CATHERINE. Okay?
ROBERT. Just a— (*More shifting around, then they both relax.*) Where did you get this bed?
CATHERINE. Garage sale at a Trappist monastery. (*Robert bursts into laughter.*) Got a hair comforter, too. (*Robert laughs even harder. Catherine looks at him.*) Jesus, Robert.
ROBERT. Sorry.
CATHERINE. Don't apologize. Apologizing is forbidden in this apartment.
ROBERT. I'll remember that. Know what they used to do?
CATHERINE. Who?
ROBERT. Monks.
CATHERINE. What.
ROBERT. Sleep with their beds at an angle, so all the wicked urges would flow out and away.
CATHERINE. Wicked urges.
ROBERT. Thank God for wicked urges.
CATHERINE. That's the best prayer I've heard in a long time.
ROBERT. Pray much?
CATHERINE. Oh, I used to. You?
ROBERT. Oh, Jesus Christ, the plane's gonna be late. That a prayer?
CATHERINE. You make love like a person who prays a lot.
ROBERT. Oh, really? This is interesting. How does a praying person make love? Stiffly? Expressionlessly?
CATHERINE. With fervor. Not expecting to get anything in return. Gently.
ROBERT. Hey, thanks.
CATHERINE. Cold?
ROBERT. No, I'm just shivering in appreciation. (*Laughs.*)
CATHERINE. What.
ROBERT. I shouldn't be enjoying myself so much.
CATHERINE. You are a praying person. (*Robert laughs again.*)

ROBERT. Catherine, I have to tell you.
CATHERINE. Yeah?
ROBERT. That I have fallen head over heels in like with you. (*Embraces her.*)
CATHERINE. (*Trying to pull away.*) Robert.
ROBERT. Let's say another prayer, c'mon, let's go for a whole rosary.
CATHERINE. Ouch.
ROBERT. (*Pulling her.*) Plenty of room on top.
CATHERINE. Rob—
ROBERT. (*Kisses her.*) Mmmmmmmm. . . .
CATHERINE. (*Pulls away firmly.*) Robert.
ROBERT. Hm?
CATHERINE. Lift your leg. (*Robert does. Catherine gets up, goes to the stereo, puts on a robe. Robert sits up.*) Whaddaya wanna hear? Webern? Sonny Rollins?
ROBERT. Is there something wrong?
CATHERINE. It's late.
ROBERT. You okay? (*Catherine turns, gives him a stern look.*) Wanna backrub?
CATHERINE. No.
ROBERT. Okay. (*Catherine puts on a record. Music: Batok's "Sonata for Solo Violin."* Catherine takes off her robe, turns toward Robert. Robert smiles. Catherine starts getting dressed.*)
CATHERINE. Chilly.
ROBERT. Winter.
CATHERINE. Right.
ROBERT. I guess I should . . . go.
CATHERINE. Yeah.
ROBERT. Oh. Well . . . (*Gets up, starts getting dressed.*) What's this?
CATHERINE. Just some Bartok. You like it?
ROBERT. Yeah, it's . . .

*See Special Note on copyright page.

CATHERINE. Interesting, yeah . . .
ROBERT. That's not what I was gonna say—
CATHERINE. Robert, I don't mean—
ROBERT. I know, I understand.
CATHERINE. Sometimes, I . . .
ROBERT. Yeah, I know what you mean.
CATHERINE. Especially at night.
ROBERT. Yeah. It was a beautiful evening.
CATHERINE. Yeah. (*Smiles.*) You look good in gooseflesh.
ROBERT. Cold in here.
CATHERINE. Landlord don't bug me about the rent, I don't bug him about the heat.
ROBERT. This is a great place.
CATHERINE. Think so?
ROBERT. Yeah, it's . . . great. (*Beat. Robert, still dressing, suddenly laughs.*)
CATHERINE. What is it with you?
ROBERT. Well . . . I'm not the world's most spontaneous guy.
CATHERINE. No.
ROBERT. But tonight, for some reason, I've been operating on instinct and chutzpah and. . . .
CATHERINE. And what do your instincts tell you?
ROBERT. That I . . . don't really want to go.
CATHERINE. You gotta go, Robert. (*Robert gets his coat, goes to Catherine and embraces her.*)
ROBERT. When?
CATHERINE. Soon.
ROBERT. Promise?
CATHERINE. Yeah.
ROBERT. Good. (*They kiss.*) Bigger kiss. (*They kiss again, then Catherine gently pulls away.*) Goodnight, Catherine.
CATHERINE. Goodnight, Robert. (*Robert starts to go, then returns, gets the two books of poetry.*)
ROBERT. Oops. (*He hesitates, smiling, then exits. Catherine gets out the Thorazine bottle, and a glass of water,*

and starts eating pills. Light fades up on Joanne.)

JOANNE. Catherine, have you been working?

CATHERINE. Working.

JOANNE. Writing.

CATHERINE. No.

JOANNE. Have you thought about getting back to work?

CATHERINE. (*Turns to look at Joanne, starts putting on a sweater.*) Well, gee, I've been busy. (*A beat.*) I don't know. This little desk has a lot of . . . magnetism, but. . . . (*Another beat.*) Actually, I've been thinking of getting a job, as a bank teller, how's that? That'd be great. Get up at eight in the morning, put on a dress make of petroleum derivatives, take the bus downtown, eat yogurt and peppermint tea for lunch. (*Pauses.*) Joanne, the poetry makes me crazy.

JOANNE. Really? That's surprising. (*Takes out the two books of poetry, puts them on her desk.*) I thought it was very lovely.

CATHERINE. Where did you get those?

JOANNE. Odegaard's.

CATHERINE. You would manage to find the one bookstore in town that carries my work. (*Beat.*) Joanne, you don't understand what I have to go through to get that stuff out. Burn it out, squeeze it out, again and again, until some seventh sense tells me it's finished. My "three A.M. dry ecstacy," as Alice so quaintly puts it. It leaves me hot, fevered and very definitely on the edge.

JOANNE. You love your work, Catherine.

CATHERINE. Well, yeah, why else would I do it, for the money? It's the only thing that makes me want to get up in the morning, it makes everything tolerable. Shit jobs, being poor, being lonely, everything gets worked out in the writing. But unfortunately it don't pay a dime and it makes me bonkers. Joanne, all I want right now is a safe, sane life.

JOANNE. It's important to be comfortable . . .

CATHERINE. Yes.

JOANNE. But I suspect that excluding this beauty from your life will create more discomfort than it prevents. (*A pause. Then Joanne stands.*) You're doing very well, Catherine. (*Exits. A brief moment, then Alice enters, opposite. Catherine turns, sees her.*)

CATHERINE. Alice.

ALICE. Do you believe this weather?

CATHERINE. Never. (*A beat. Catherine goes to Alice, concerned.*) What's . . . ?

ALICE. I'm sorry about lunch, I was a shit. Okay? Because I feel very passionately about your work, so when you told me you were quitting, which I still don't belive, I saw red. Your work's about the only thing I still feel passionately about, God help me. Where you been?

CATHERINE. Have you been waiting for me? Out here?

ALICE. So you forgive me, right? I'm an asshole and you always have to forgive me. Jesus, it's cold.

CATHERINE. Well, come on in.

ALICE. More than anything, I don't want you back in that hospital. That was just . . . too much, I can't take that. I need you.

CATHERINE. So do I.

ALICE. So the poetry makes you crazy. Well, okay, you're the expert, I guess. I swear to God, sometimes, I get nostalgic for last week.

CATHERINE. Alice.

ALICE. What.

CATHERINE. Come in before you collapse.

ALICE. Well, okay, sure, if you want me to.

CATHERINE. Come on. (*They enter the apartment.*)

ALICE. (*Looking around.*) Oh my God.

CATHERINE. Hm?

ALICE. It's clean. Lookit this, you can see the floor. They teach you to make beds in the hospital?

CATHERINE. Cocoa?

ALICE. What?

CATHERINE. Want some—?

ALICE. Cocoa. (*Glances toward the kitchen.*) No. (*Beat: Alice sits.*) How's Robert?

CATHERINE. Who?

ALICE. Hey, c'mon, he was over last night and I'll tell you, that boy's got the serious hots for you. And I also ascertained that he doesn't know about the "big S," which was awkward, you shit, because I had to signal Ed to keep his mouth shut with my eyebrows. And you know how subtle he is. It was exhausting. You afraid you're gonna scare him away?

CATHERINE. Ed?

ALICE. Ed's gone.

CATHERINE. Gone?

ALICE. Again. We had a long, rational conversation about his drinking and he poured a fifth of Jim Beam down the toilet and this morning he was gone. He never gets arrested and we have separate checking accounts, so I'm not too worried. This is the first time he's done it in the middle of a project, though.

CATHERINE. You all right?

ALICE. No. (*Beat.*) You know what I think about Robert, though, that he'd find the idea of the schizophrenia very . . . sexy, y'know? He's the kinda guy who thinks everybody's crazy except him. Ed admires him a lot. I think you should—

CATHERINE. Alice.

ALICE. Right, none of my business. Welcome home and everything. I think you're the only person in the world who'll listen to me blather. Hey, whaddaya call that stuff in the loony bin, beads and baskets, and—?

CATHERINE. Occupational Therapy.

ALICE. Right.

CATHERINE. OT.

ALICE. You want some OT? I'm up to my ass in bad poetry and godawful novels and putrid verse plays about Pocahontas. Wanna read it? Read it all? Be my "editorial assistant?" I'll pay you even. Oh, Christ, listen to me. Part time. Okay?

CATHERINE. Okay.
ALICE. I promise not to rag you about the writing. Who cares if it's gone. All ten of our readers'll be pissed but to hell with'em, we'll still be working together. Friends, Okay?
CATHERINE. (*Looking away, softly.*) Okay.
ALICE. I don't care about anything else. (*Beat.*) Well, look, come by tomorrow, any time after three, I'm in meetings until then. Okay? Catherine?
CATHERINE. Okay. Alice, I gotta. . . .
ALICE. (*Stands, puts on her coat.*) Me too. See you tomorrow. (*Goes to the door.*) You okay?
CATHERINE. Are you?
ALICE. (*Laughs.*) See you, babe. (*Exits. A moment: Catherine standing in the apartment, alone. Robert enters, with wine.*)
ROBERT. What?
CATHERINE. Hm?
ROBERT. Whaddaya mean, line?
CATHERINE. Well, key, whatever. Area. And the rest of the ensemble moves in relation to it so sometimes you hear the violin and sometimes you don't, depending.
ROBERT. Depending on what?
CATHERINE. What?
ROBERT. I don't know what you're talking about.
CATHERINE. You hated the concert.
ROBERT. No.
CATHERINE. Admit it.
ROBERT. No, goddamit, I liked it, I really did. I might've had to go through life never knowing cellos could sound like that.
CATHERINE. Robert, before I'm done with you, you'll be eating twentieth century music with a spoon.
ROBERT. Before you're "done," eh? I can't wait. (*Catherine is looking for an album.*) Please, none of that demolition derby synthesizer stuff. Or that hog slaughterhouse vocal music.
CATHERINE. (*Smiles evilly, holds up an album.*) This

one'll make your eyeballs vibrate.

ROBERT. Oh God. (*Catherine puts on the album. Pause. Then music: slow, melodic, very beautiful saxophone music — Sonny Rollins' variations on Ellington's "In a Sentimental Mood."**) All right. (*Catherine smiles.*) C'mere. (*An embrace, quite passionate. Robert puts his hands under her sweater.*) God, your skin. Gooseflesh. I got a cure for that. Let's — (*He tries to pull her to the bed. Catherine breaks away, gently.*)

CATHERINE. I take it you like the music.

ROBERT. (*Laughs.*) It's pretty interesting, yeah.

CATHERINE. (*In kitchen, getting the corkscrew.*) Here. (*Tosses it to Robert, who catches it, starts to open the wine.*)

ROBERT. How 'bout some coffee cups, or maybe a couple soupladles?

CATHERINE. (*Gets two coffee cups.*) They're even clean.

ROBERT. (*After a pause.*) Alice says you two're working on a new book.

CATHERINE. When'd she say that?

ROBERT. Oh, the other night. Anyway, could I —

CATHERINE. It's not going very well. Don't look at me like that, you're breaking my heart.

ROBERT. God, what a trip it must be, to be able to write like that, to . . . do that. I spend so much time looking at computer printouts, growth projections, stock tables, it's so refreshing to come here, to a place with. . . .

CATHERINE. Filth.

ROBERT. Atmosphere. Your atmosphere, you. I really wanna read your new stuff. What's wrong?

CATHERINE. Robert, I don't want to talk about my work. (*Beat.*) Let's just listen to music and sip wine.

ROBERT. Are you having problems?

CATHERINE. Let's talk about your work.

ROBERT. No.

*See Special Note on copyright page.

CATHERINE. What is a stock, anyway? I've never understood—
ROBERT. No. My work's interesting, sometimes. Plus the power hit you get from playing with other people's money. The money you get from playing with other people's money. (*Suddenly stands.*) God, I'd like to quit.
CATHERINE. Take up watercolors.
ROBERT. Right. Movies on Monday afternoons, that's always been a fantasy of mine. Actually, I don't know what I'd do. (*A beat, smiles.*) Make love with you, constantly. (*Goes to her, embraces her.*) God, I love making love with you. It makes everything disappear, for a delicious few moments, everything's gone. God, I love you.
CATHERINE. (*Trying to pull away.*) Robert, I don't know what that means.
ROBERT. You're the most exciting woman I've ever met. I love you.
CATHERINE. (*Firmly.*) Robert. (*Robert stands once again, moves away, getting rather agitated.*)
ROBERT. Fuck, I'm sorry.
CATHERINE. Don't apologize.
ROBERT. I don't know what's wrong with me.
CATHERINE. There's nothing—
ROBERT. Catherine, I—
CATHERINE. Robert. (*Beat.*) Sometimes, you're like a young boy.
ROBERT. (*Bitterly.*) Thanks.
CATHERINE. It's true. Robert, you're a very kind, very honest—
ROBERT. Oh, yeah, I know, as nice a guy as you'll find anywhere, a real human bean, good ole—
CATHERINE. It's a very rare quality! Think about what you have, Robert, not about what you don't have. Or can't have. (*Pause. Robert moves away.*) Robert, I . . . Robert, there are a lot of things you don't understand.
ROBERT. Yeah? Really?

CATHERINE. Really. (*Robert pours more wine, shakily, sits at the table, obviously upset, trying to make up his mind to say something. Catherine watches him for a moment, then finally asks:*) What is it?
ROBERT. I'm . . . going to San Francisco on Monday.
CATHERINE. Business?
ROBERT. Yeah.
CATHERINE. Oh, well, that'll be nice. It's a beautiful city, or so I hear. How long will you be gone?
ROBERT. Four weeks.
CATHERINE. Well, that'll be nice.
ROBERT. I'm going to miss you, really miss—
CATHERINE. You travel a lot?
ROBERT. I do, yeah. Since I don't have a family, I do a lot of the firm's out of town business. Plus I travel on my own time quite a bit.
CATHERINE. Sounds nice.
ROBERT. Catherine—
CATHERINE. Is it true the world is a huge airline terminal, surrounded by slums?
ROBERT. I was thinking you could come with me.
CATHERINE. Oh, Robert.
ROBERT. I've got more money than I know what to do with, you know that, it wouldn't be a problem. And it is a beautiful city.
CATHERINE. I know. Robert, I . . . don't know what to say.
ROBERT. You wouldn't have to stay for four weeks. Unless you wanted to. (*Pauses.*) And maybe . . . a change of scenery would help you with your new book. I mean, if you're having problems. . . . (*Catherine tries to stifle a laugh, turns away, then laughs out loud.*) Great. Make me feel like an asshole, I love it.
CATHERINE. (*Patiently.*) Robert, we live in two different worlds.
ROBERT. I don't believe that.

CATHERINE. You don't know the first thing about me.
ROBERT. Oh, I see, we live in two completely separate places, nothing in common, right? You keep cutting youself off like that, you'll suffer, and your work'll suffer, too!
CATHERINE. (*Laughs.*) Oh, Jesus Christ!
ROBERT. I'm an expert at cutting myself off from the world, I know what I'm talking about.
CATHERINE. (*Angry.*) And what'm I gonna do in San Francisco with an "investment consultant," eat steaks!?
ROBERT. Whaddaya gonna do here? Listen to weird music and brood about the book you're not writing!?
CATHERINE. (*Turns away.*) Robert!!!
ROBERT. Oh, shit. Catherine, I'm— (*Tries to touch her but she pulls away.*) Are you . . . ? (*Tense beat. Then Catherine abruptly goes to the stereo, rejects the record.*)
CATHERINE. You better go. Go on, make your escape, before I drink your blood. You're always glad to leave this place, so—
ROBERT. Cath—
CATHERINE. You don't know how lucky you are to have your computer printouts and your three piece suits and your money and your anger you can get your teeth into without going insane! (*A beat, calms herself.*) You best stay away from me, Robert, I'm poison. Believe me.
ROBERT. Are you okay?
CATHERINE. Robert!
ROBERT. All right. (*Reluctantly gets his coat and exits. Catherine gets out her pill tray, starts slamming pill bottles down on the table.*)
CATHERINE. This is what I am. This is my life. This is the world I live in. This is why I can't go to San Francisco. This is why I can't write. This is what I am. (*Light fades up on Joanne.*)
JOANNE. Do you realize how angry you sound?
CATHERINE. Goddamit. . . . (*Clenches her fists, bows her head. Spot fades up on Alice.*)

JOANNE. Catherine.
ALICE. Catherine.
JOANNE. Catherine.
ALICE. I can't separate you from your work. It's inside you, you'll never get away from it, no matter what you do, whether you write it down or not.
CATHERINE. (*To Joanne.*) "I'm an angry young woman." "Oh? And why are you angry?" "I don't know, that's what makes me angry."
JOANNE. I'm unimpressed.
CATHERINE. Good, be unimpressed, it suits you.
ALICE. It was gonna be your best work, you know that, don't you?
CATHERINE. I can't think about that now, Alice, can't you understand, the voices are—
ALICE. Whatever you have, it's something so rare.
CATHERINE. Thank God.
ALICE. You have a voice.
CATHERINE. No, the voices are somewhere else, they have nothing to do with me.
JOANNE. (*Rapidly.*) Do you recognize the voices, are they always in an understandable language, do they mock you—
ALICE. (*Slowly, overlapping Joanne.*) It's . . . so . . . beautiful . . .
JOANNE. —yell at you? Are they ever your own voice? (*The phone rings. A pause. Phone rings again, and again. The light on Joanne and Alice slowly fades. A spot fades up on Robert. Catherine, finally, answers her phone.*)
CATHERINE. Hello.
ROBERT. I know I apologize too much. So I'd like to take this opportunity to apologize for the apologizing I'm going to do now and for any apologizing I may do in the future. You there?
CATHERINE. Yes.
ROBERT. I'm sorry about the other night. I had no right to create that kind of pressure.

CATHERINE. You're creating pressure now.
ROBERT. I'll be back on the ninth. If you want, you can call me. I . . . hope you will.
CATHERINE. Fly safely, Robert.
ROBERT. You, too. (*Robert's light fades. After a beat, Catherine hangs up the phone. She goes to the stereo, puts on a record. Music: an Elliott Carter quartet: slow, with harsh melodies.* Catherine goes to the bed, rips a blanket off the covers, wraps herself in it, sits on the floor, huddled. Tableau. Then the lights fade to blackout.*)

END OF ACT ONE

*See Special Note on copyright page.

ACT TWO

Darkness. *Music: Philip Glass' "Music in Similar Motion,"* quite loud. The music increases dramatically in volume, then suddenly cuts out. Lights fade up quickly: Catherine is sitting at her writing desk, caught in a small pool of light.*

CATHERINE. They used to fly at me. (*Beat.*) Like bullets. Like bullets, they'd mushroom inside me, expanding and twisting, growing, always making a bigger hole leaving. (*Pauses, then laughs.*) No, not like that at all, nothing like that. (*Beat.*) Music. Yeah, more like music. Bartok poems, Crumb poems, Coltrane poems, Ives poems, even Beethoven poems when I was young. Younger. (*Beat.*) Always in a woman's voice. (*Beat.*) Percussion poems. Saxophone poems, always about the night. Poem for— (*Tapping on objects on the desk.*) —number two pencil, empty wine bottle and broken coffee cup. Solo violin poems, about flying. Bach partita poems. Poem for unaccompanied girls chorus. (*Beat.*) Fly at me. White dreamvoicemusicbullets, from the darkness.
JOANNE. (*Not visible.*) And is it so frightening?
CATHERINE. I don't know. (*Beat.*) No. I wish it were.
JOANNE. Voices?
CATHERINE. Sometimes they . . . demand to be written down.

*See Special Note on copyright page.

JOANNE. So . . . why not?
CATHERINE. And I feel cold without it.
JOANNE. Are you frightened?
CATHERINE. Heck no. Not with my faithful pal Thorazine standing by.
JOANNE. You love your work, Catherine. I can feel the passion in your voice when you talk about it.
CATHERINE. Passionate hatred.
JOANNE. No.
CATHERINE. Lately, I've tried to be frightened, but . . .
JOANNE. You can defeat the voices—
CATHERINE. (*Overlaps her.*) And the colors, the dreams, the music—
JOANNE. —without giving in to them. (*Catherine picks up a postcard. Spot fades up on Robert.*)
ROBERT. Dear Catherine. They say many artists live in this city. This is an exageration. There was an artist here in 1969 but she disappeared, unaccountably. Wine is too strong and the bread in restaurants smells of your body. Miss you. Robert. (*Beat. Robert's light slowly fades.*)
CATHERINE. God, I want it back so bad. The hot taste of the coffee, the cramp in my wrist, the pounding in my heart, the music of the words, the energy, the way they fly at me.
JOANNE. You must learn to accept your illness. It's part of you. Don't pretend it's not real, don't fight your awareness of it.
CATHERINE. Do I want it to stay away?
JOANNE. You are stronger than the illness, I know you are. (*A spot up again on Robert.*)
ROBERT. Dear Catherine.
CATHERINE. Please, no.
ROBERT. This is a strange city. The night air is obscenely warm and filled with the sounds of birds. The people I work with have holes for eyes. I cannot open the windows of my hotel room. Please forgive me for writing so much, I can't help it. Love. Robert. (*Robert's light fades.*)

JOANNE. Symptoms?

CATHERINE. No dreams, no colors, I sleep like a corpse. I'm doing very well.

JOANNE. You're doing very well.

CATHERINE. Doing very well. (*Catherine crosses to Joanne's area, sits. Lights concentrate on them. Beat, as Joanne regards Catherine for a moment.*)

JOANNE. (*Looking in her notes.*) Well, Catherine, I think we can cut our meetings down to once a week.

CATHERINE. What? But Joanne—

JOANNE. I know you're—

CATHERINE. I'm sorry if I, I dunno, said the wrong thing, but—

JOANNE. It's not that, you know it.

CATHERINE. Once a week is still a lot, I know, but— (*Stops herself. A pause.*) Fridays?

JOANNE. I think Wednesdays would be better. I'm doing a seminar at the university, every other Friday.

CATHERINE. Going to make for some long weekends.

JOANNE. I have confidence in you. And you can always call me. I'm available for you, you know that.

CATHERINE. Well . . .

JOANNE. See you next Wednesday. (*Catherine goes back to the apartment. Joanne's light fades. Alice enters.*)

CATHERINE. Hi.

ALICE. Hi. I stopped by.

CATHERINE. Yes, you did.

ALICE. I got your note about that schoolgirl novel which I read last night, and hated.

CATHERINE. You read it last night? All of it?

ALICE. How long does it take to read a bad novel?

CATHERINE. I liked it.

ALICE. Yeah, I know how it is, when you read all that junk, it's exhilarating to get something that's not kitchen-sink-reeking-of-raw-yellow-onions, but you should try—

CATHERINE. I especially liked the sense of color in the

book. Browns, earth colors.

ALICE. I passed it to Bill.

CATHERINE. He'll like it.

ALICE. He'll love it. Well . . .

CATHERINE. Fine, how are you?

ALICE. I don't know. I haven't seen you for a while.

CATHERINE. Been busy.

ALICE. You?

CATHERINE. I know, my busy is your suspended animation.

ALICE. (*Hesitates, then forced-casual.*) Listen, I'm glad I caught you. Robert's coming home today. (*Short pause.*) Robert. Puppy dog eyes.

CATHERINE. Really.

ALICE. Catherine.

CATHERINE. Hm?

ALICE. I told him.

CATHERINE. You . . . ?

ALICE. About the schizophrenia, and about the hospital, the Thorazine, the shrinks. I told him everything. I spilled your guts. (*Beat.*) Ed got a call from him yesterday, he's flying in this afternoon. He had to stay an extra week on accounta some client checked out so they had to spend all his money before estate taxes, something like that. Ed talked to him. He's agonizing to see you. Apparently, he's been wandering around San Francisco, bumping into trees. (*Pauses.*) You hate me?

CATHERINE. (*Pause.*) No.

ALICE. I don't blame you. But he was upset. I figured, as a friend, he had a right to know how deep the water was he was drowning in. You shoulda been the one to tell him, Catherine.

CATHERINE. I know.

ALICE. (*Stands, paces.*) This place feels so different. I like it. What'd you do?

CATHERINE. I changed.

ALICE. (*After a beat.*) There was one part of the book I liked.
CATHERINE. The car crash after the sex.
ALICE. (*Laughs.*) Got a piece of paper in that desk?
CATHERINE. Yeah?
ALICE. Write this down: Thursday the twentysixth, one P.M.
CATHERINE. What's that?
ALICE. Well, we're gonna publish that Gertrude Stein biography and that's the first staff meeting on it. Can you make it? Just what the world needs, another Gertie Stein book. (*Beat.*) Because: I like having you around, I value your opinion, I trust you.
CATHERINE. Even though I like schoolgirl novels?
ALICE. Oh, I hate everything. That's why I have Bill, who loves everything. And now you, someone with taste. (*Beat.*) You don't have to take the job.
CATHERINE. It's a "job"?
ALICE. (*Hesitates.*) Yeah, it's a job. One of my problems is that I'm so fucking territorial about my work, so don't feel you have to grovel and weep in gratitude, even though that may seem to be what I want, but nevertheless, I wish you'd say something 'cause I'm starting to babble here.
CATHERINE. Thursday the twenty-sixth.
ALICE. Well, read the book, first. Stop by and pick it up. Make sure I'm gonna be around, I wanna see you.
CATHERINE. Okay, thanks.
ALICE. We're gonna be working together again. Far out.
CATHERINE. Well, yes, but—
ALICE. (*Looking at her watch.*) Shit. (*Starts putting on her coat.*)
CATHERINE. My love to Ed?
ALICE. Who? (*At the door, turns.*) My love to Robert.
CATHERINE. If I see him.
ALICE. You'll see him. Ciao. (*Exits. Pause: Catherine picks*

up the two postcards, rereads them. Light fades up on Joanne.)

JOANNE. And if it comes back, you have your friend, you have the Thorazine, you have—

CATHERINE. I have my list.

JOANNE. Continue taking the Thorazine at—

CATHERINE. I have my list.

JOANNE. You're doing very well. *(Joanne's light fades. A spot fades up on Robert. Catherine's phone rings.)*

CATHERINE. *(Answers it.)* Hello.

ROBERT. Catherine. *(Pause.)* Catherine, it's—

CATHERINE. Hello, Robert.

ROBERT. Hi.

CATHERINE. How you doing?

ROBERT. Fine. How you doing?

CATHERINE. You're not in San Francisco, are you?

ROBERT. No, I'm not.

CATHERINE. Did you have a good time?

ROBERT. I had an interesting time, very interesting.

CATHERINE. Was it foggy?

ROBERT. Yes. *(Laughs.)*

CATHERINE. What.

ROBERT. Nothing, nothing. Listen, I bought us a present.

CATHERINE. You shouldn't have.

ROBERT. I can deliver it at any time. Or not deliver it at all.

CATHERINE. What is it?

ROBERT. When would be a good time?

CATHERINE. Oh, now would be a good time.

ROBERT. I'll unpack later. *(His light fades; he exits. Catherine stands quietly for a moment, than laughs. She looks around, makes a meagre effort to tidy the apartment. She sees the pill tray, laughs, puts it away.)*

JOANNE. *(In darkness.)* Continue taking the Thorazine at—

CATHERINE. Joanne, I have my list.

JOANNE. You're doing very well. (*Stands.*) See you Wednesday. (*Joanne exits. Catherine puts on a record. Music: early Coltrane; slow and bluesy.* Robert enters, carrying a case of wine and a smaller box from a gift shop.*)
CATHERINE. Hi. Come on in. (*Robert enters the apartment. Beat: they look at each other, smilingly.*) That wine?
ROBERT. Hm? Oh, yes. A young, arrogant, almost snitty, but still quite affectionate Cabernet Sauvignon. I bought it at one of those Napa Valley wineries at the end of a long gravel road. Corkscrew. (*Opens the case, takes out a bottle of red wine. Catherine gives him a corkscrew and Robert opens the bottle, sniffs it.*) Mm. We should let it breathe, half an hour at least.
CATHERINE. (*Reaches for the bottle.*) Gimme the bottle.
ROBERT. (*Pulls the bottle away.*) Catherine, I know it's disgustingly bourgeois, but this is wine that requires glasses. (*Opens the small box, takes out two crystal wine glasses.*)
CATHERINE. (*Laughs.*) Oh God. (*Robert ostentatiously pours wine, gives her a glass, offers a toast.*)
ROBERT. To . . . ?
CATHERINE. To you. (*They drink.*) God.
ROBERT. Good, eh? It's like you can taste the rich California sun in it.
CATHERINE. (*Takes another sip.*) God.
ROBERT. Yeah, it's a find.
CATHERINE. Wow.
ROBERT. Some more?
CATHERINE. (*Holds out her glass.*) Yeah. How much?
ROBERT. Oh . . .
CATHERINE. C'mon.
ROBERT. Never mind.
CATHERINE. Tell me.
ROBERT. You don't wanna know.
CATHERINE. I wanna—

*See Special Note on copyright page.

ROBERT. Three hundred eighty.

CATHERINE. For . . . twelve bottles?

ROBERT. Life is short. (*They sip their wine.*) Can we . . . sit?

CATHERINE. Oh, sure. (*Moves books and other debris, and they sit.*)

ROBERT. So how are you?

CATHERINE. Good. You? We did this part on the phone.

ROBERT. It's . . . really good to see you. You're looking very beautiful.

CATHERINE. So are you.

ROBERT. Thanks.

CATHERINE. Weather's been awful.

ROBERT. Yeah?

CATHERINE. I suppose it was nice in California.

ROBERT. Yes, weatherwise, anyway.

CATHERINE. Hm. Cryptic remark.

ROBERT. Catherine—

CATHERINE. Robert—

ROBERT. I'm really—

CATHERINE. Look, Robert. I know you know.

ROBERT. What?

CATHERINE. You know. About the schizophrenia, about the hospital, the Thorazine. I know you know.

ROBERT. Alice told me not to tell you she told me.

CATHERINE. She told me she told you.

ROBERT. She did.

CATHERINE. Yeah. (*Short pause, then they both laugh shyly.*)

ROBERT. Catherine, all that stuff before I left—

CATHERINE. No apologizing!

ROBERT. I'm not gonna apologize, I'm gonna explain.

CATHERINE. No. No explaining, no apologizing. No fretting about the future.

ROBERT. (*Smiles weakly.*) House rules, eh?

CATHERINE. We may not have time. (*Pause. Catherine*

and Robert look at each other for a long moment.)

ROBERT. Put on a record. (*Catherine complies. Music: Gary Peacock/Keith Jarret's "Tales of Another."* Another moment, then they embrace, passionately. Lights blackout.*)

CATHERINE. (*Speaking in the darkness.*) I had this ritual when I was a girl. I'd sit on my bed, all huddled up, very still, till I could feel myself starting to doze off. Then, I'd start saying my name, over and over, like a mantra. I'd get this really strange buzz, but not physical at all, and I could feel my eyes getting wider and wider. (*Lights have been slowly fading up: Catherine and Robert are in bed.*) Then: nothing. Nothing. I'd come to and hours would have passed.

ROBERT. Were you sleeping?

CATHERINE. Maybe.

ROBERT. I wish I could do that. Disappear.

CATHERINE. Do you really?

ROBERT. (*Slight pause.*) As long as I was sure I could come back.

CATHERINE. That's the catch.

ROBERT. Is that what happens when you . . . get sick? You disappear?

CATHERINE. Hours, days, weeks. Gone.

ROBERT. God.

CATHERINE. And writing, too. Sometimes. Not so much any more, not since I became a "professional." It used to be great. Scribble, scribble and hours disappear. When I was a girl I had boxes of notebooks. The first time I went to the hospital my mother threw them away.

ROBERT. Ohhh . . .

CATHERINE. Good riddance. (*Beat.*) You know what part of you I kept thinking about, all the while you were gone?

ROBERT. Part of my body?

CATHERINE. Yeah.

ROBERT. What?

*See Special Note on copyright page.

CATHERINE. Your hands. You have the softest, sexiest hands. Businessman's hands. (*Kisses his hands.*)

ROBERT. Mmmmmmmmoooooohhhhhh, God, Catherine. (*Embraces her.*) You don't know how I missed you. Yours was the only face I ever saw.

CATHERINE. How horrible.

ROBERT. One day, I drank four martinis at lunch. They do that in San Francisco, they take fashionably long, alcoholic lunches. I told 'em all about my divorce. Focusing primarily on the night my wife left me, when I tried to smash her in the face with my corporate law textbook and broke my little finger on her forehead when she ducked. (*Pauses.*) The way we both laughed. The way I cried when she left me alone at the hospital. How poor we were. Students. (*A beat.*) I don't know how long I can keep this life up, Catherine. The people I have to work with, the face I have to wear. I wanna just bury myself in you.

CATHERINE. Robert, God, no, not in me.

ROBERT. What? I'm—

CATHERINE. It's dangerous. Jesus, I don't think you know how dangerous this is. (*Gets up, quickly, and puts on a robe.*)

ROBERT. Where you going?

CATHERINE. (*Gets out her pill tray.*) Give us this night our nightly T. (*Starts taking pills out of the bottles.*) Don't watch.

ROBERT. You have to eat all those?

CATHERINE. Mostly vitamins. (*Holds up the Thorazine.*) This is the heavy artillery.

ROBERT. Thorazine?

CATHERINE. God's gift to the gifted. I didn't have this stuff, you'd be peeling me off the ceiling with a crowbar. (*Swallows some pills.*)

ROBERT. What happens? I mean, when the schizophrenia comes, what're your . . . ?

CATHERINE. Symptoms.

ROBERT. Yeah.

CATHERINE. The usual: voices, hallucinations, celestial choirs, no sleep. My pet hallucination is feeling my body melt away, dissolve into hot blood, then pink steam, then nothing. The shrinks all think that one's great, they're fascinated by it. I scream a lot, I choke on my tongue.

ROBERT. Jesus.

CATHERINE. It's dangerous, Robert, I'm telling you, people like me should be put away.

ROBERT. Don't try to scare me away, Catherine, because you can't.

CATHERINE. It can happen to me at any time. This isn't some storybook poet's-garret-white-wine-in-the-moonlight— (*Stops herself. A silence, as Catherine eats more pills.*)

ROBERT. Does the Thorazine help?

CATHERINE. Usually. It's not as bad as it could be. I'm what's known as a high function schizophrenic. I'm lucky.

ROBERT. You still have some symptoms?

CATHERINE. Voices, sometimes.

ROBERT. Really? Do you have any symptoms right now?

CATHERINE. (*Smiles.*) Only you.

ROBERT. What do the voices say?

CATHERINE. (*Laughs uncomfortably.*) Robert. I try not to . . . listen to them.

ROBERT. How does it affect your writing?

CATHERINE. Interesting questions, Robert. (*Quick beat.*) I'm gonna cut the poetry nonsense loose. The world can't afford poets any more, there's not enough time, or enough—

ROBERT. Don't talk like that!

CATHERINE. Don't romanticize this stuff, don't romanticize my poetry, my apartment, my illness, me. You'll get us both in trouble.

ROBERT. Aren't you writing?

CATHERINE. Trying. But . . . (*Pauses.*) Maybe you should go home.

ROBERT. No.

CATHERINE. I've just taken my meds and I'm about to sleep the sleep of the dead.
ROBERT. You really miss it.
CATHERINE. Yeah. God, Robert, I do.
ROBERT. Well, maybe you are writing, even if you don't know it.
CATHERINE. What?
ROBERT. Well, it's probably like athletics, right? You gotta build your stamina, develop your . . . faculties, before you can really play the game. Train. Right? Maybe that's what you're doing now. And pretty soon, you'll be . . . writing.
CATHERINE. Oh, Robert.
ROBERT. (*Angrily.*) Well, I don't know what else to say. I just want you to . . . write.
CATHERINE. You don't know how dangerous this is. (*Beat: they look at each other. Lights fade. Lights fade up again: Catherine, still wearing her robe, is sitting at her desk, writing. Light fades up on Joanne.*)
JOANNE. So.
CATHERINE. Hm?
JOANNE. How's the writing going?
CATHERINE. (*Laughs.*) You can read it in my face? Yeah, I'm writing, and it's awful, It's rough. Sketchy. I'm working on some old, unfinished stuff, haven't started anything new. Maybe I won't. I don't know if it's going to work.
JOANNE. Why do you say that?
CATHERINE. Maybe I let it go this time. Maybe I can't get it back.
JOANNE. You sound almost hopeful.
CATHERINE. No, it's there. It's just . . . shy.
JOANNE. Shy?
CATHERINE. It's there. (*Finishes dressing, then crosses to Joanne, sits.*) Joanne? Can I reduce the Thorazine? (*Beat. Joanne looks at her for a moment, then starts writing in the notes.*) Joanne.
JOANNE. I don't think that would be a good idea. We're

still on rocky ground, Catherine. I understand your impatience and I think it's a good sign—

CATHERINE. Like all the other "signs."

JOANNE. But you'll have to live with the Thorazine for quite a while longer. Are you dissatisfied with your progress?

CATHERINE. No, that's just it. I feel stronger now than I have in a long time.

JOANNE. Then why so impatient?

CATHERINE. It's more than that, it's a question of who and what I am! (*Pauses.*) The stuff I'm doing is awful.

JOANNE. And you blame the medication.

CATHERINE. Try eating five hundred milligrams of Thorazine every day and see how effectively you work. I'm tired of dragging my ass out of bed at eleven every morning, tired of being a "mental patient."

JOANNE. You want to be normal?

CATHERINE. Yeah. (*A beat.*) Well, I wanna feel normal, pretend to be normal, live some sort of life! I'm tired of feeling like some fucking circus geek! Shit. (*Covers her face with her hands.*) I wait a whole week to see you and now this.

JOANNE. Have you shown your new poems to Alice?

CATHERINE. You don't let up, do you? No, I haven't. She'll kill me.

JOANNE. Why?

CATHERINE. Because they're awful! (*Pauses.*) She gave me a promotion. I don't think she wants me to be a poet any more, she just wants me around.

JOANNE. And Robert?

CATHERINE. He's back, God help me.

JOANNE. Is that why you want to cut down on the Thorazine, because you're afraid it makes you less appealing to Robert?

CATHERINE. (*Stares at Joanne, surprised. A pause.*) He's crazier'n I am.

JOANNE. Your illness is just that, an illness, something you can defeat. It has nothing to do with what you are.

Catherine. It's possible that you'll never be normal, not in an ordinary sense. You have a very serious illness. But that doesn't mean that you can't have a life. A rewarding life. Like most schizophrenics, you are very gifted, and very sensitive.
CATHERINE. So I should count my blessings? (*Beat.*) Oh God. I don't know if I can do it.
JOANNE. There'll be more poetry.
CATHERINE. Is that a threat?
JOANNE. No. (*Catherine stands.*) Catherine, you're doing—
CATHERINE. Very well, I know.
JOANNE. I'm proud of you. (*Catherine exits. Joanne's light fades. Catherine goes to the apartment, puts a sheaf of poems into a manila envelope, then goes to the bare stage area, sits in a chair. After a moment, Alice enters, briskly, carrying a book length manuscript.*)
ALICE. Hi, babe.
CATHERINE. Hi, Alice.
ALICE. I made you wait.
CATHERINE. It's all right.
ALICE. (*Gives Catherine the ms.*) Well, here it is, in all its indolent splendor. *Gertrude Stein: A Life.* Bill says it's the best thing since beer. That's a copy, so feel free to get Mickey Mouse.
CATHERINE. Get . . . ?
ALICE. Spelling, punctuation, grammar, etcetera. Word choice. I wanna get it through design and into galleys by the end of next month. Know anything about Gertrude Stein?
CATHERINE. Not a thing.
ALICE. Good. Now look. I wanna make this as gossipy as possible, so we'll be looking at cuts in the analysis sections which I find even duller than Stein's work. I've marked—
CATHERINE. Alice.
ALICE. What?
CATHERINE. I've got something for you.
ALICE. Yeah?

CATHERINE. Here. (*Catherine gives Alice her poems. Alice looks at her, then opens the envelope, takes out the poems.*)
ALICE. Good God.
CATHERINE. I've been . . . nervous about showing them to you.
ALICE. When'd you do these?
CATHERINE. Recently. They're rough.
ALICE. Yeah?
CATHERINE. I haven't . . . gotten my stride back yet, I dunno. Alice, don't read 'em now, wait till later.
ALICE. You okay?
CATHERINE. Please stop asking me that.
ALICE. It's just a question from a friend. Before, you told me the writing made you bonkers, so now you're writing and I'm wondering—
CATHERINE. I'm fine.
ALICE. You gonna be able to work with me on the Stein book?
CATHERINE. (*Slight pause.*) I told you I would.
ALICE. (*After a beat.*) I marked the chapters that need cutting. We'll need to present a united front to the author who may, will, shit bricks. Preliminary meeting with her is . . . (*Looks at Catherine.*) Listening?
CATHERINE. Yeah. Thursday the—
ALICE. That's the staff meeting. Monday the first, ten A.M. That okay?
CATHERINE. Fine.
ALICE. (*Pauses, looks away.*) I'm about to ax the secretary. Seems like I go through about four a year. So if I'm a bit . . .
CATHERINE. It's okay.
ALICE. You're writing, eh?
CATHERINE. Yeah.
ALICE. Well. . . . I gotta go to a meeting.
CATHERINE. Read in good health.
ALICE. You too. Bye, babe. (*Exits. Catherine returns to the*

apartment, sits. Robert enters, knocks on the door.)

CATHERINE. Robert?

ROBERT. Yeah, hi, it's me. (*Enters.*)

CATHERINE. God, I'm glad you're here. (*Hugs him.*) Mm. You're chilled. What'd you do, walk?

ROBERT. Yeah, it's great.

CATHERINE. It's cold.

ROBERT. Crisp. It's nice.

CATHERINE. You look strange.

ROBERT. I am strange. (*A beat, then Robert laughs.*) Let's eat steaks. Big juicy hunks of semi-raw cow.

CATHERINE. You're making my mouth water.

ROBERT. Yeah?

CATHERINE. Listen, I got a surprise for you.

ROBERT. Let's go eat, really, I'm starved.

CATHERINE. I wanna show you—

ROBERT. Don't you get stir crazy in this apartment? It's hot in here, Jesus.

CATHERINE. The landlord is in an atypically generous mood tonight.

ROBERT. I got good news.

CATHERINE. Yeah?

ROBERT. I think I quit my job today.

CATHERINE. (*Surprised.*) You . . . ?

ROBERT. I think so, yeah.

CATHERINE. You think so. Either you did, or you didn't.

ROBERT. The chairman and I had a discussion and he asked if perhaps I wasn't "dissatisfied" with the firm.

CATHERINE. And you said . . . ?

ROBERT. I said I was as happy as a pig in shit, but I think he was politely asking me to resign.

CATHERINE. You okay?

ROBERT. I'm fine, I'm terrific, happier than a pig in shit. Kiss me you fool. (*Catherine hesitates. Robert goes to her, hug and kisses her.*) Mm. God, I hate that oak and leather office, fucking wool tweed secretaries. Let's celebrate, c'mon.

Pour some of that incredible wine.

CATHERINE. Take off your coat. (*Robert removes his coat. Catherine pour wine into coffee cups, hands one to Robert.*) A cup of wine.

ROBERT. I've been thinking about this wine all day. Something that makes sense.

CATHERINE. (*Offers a toast.*) To time on your hands.

ROBERT. Yeah.

CATHERINE. You'll get into being unemployed. It's the new thing, you know.

ROBERT. Let's get away from this shitty gray city. Mexico. You wanna—?

CATHERINE. Robert.

ROBERT. Why not, you so busy here? Shit, forget I said that. I'm sorry.

CATHERINE. Don't—

ROBERT. And forget I said I'm sorry. I'll never say it again, I promise. (*A beat. Catherine looks at Robert for a moment, then suddenly goes to the stereo.*)

CATHERINE. John Cage?

ROBERT. No.

CATHERINE. Anthony Braxton?

ROBERT. No, please.

CATHERINE. Charley Parker?

ROBERT. Cath—

CATHERINE. Kingston Trio?

ROBERT. No music, not tonight, please. I think if I hear any of that shit I'll go nuts.

CATHERINE. To coin a phrase. (*Another, longer, beat. Catherine looks at Robert closely, really concerned. Robert is obviously very agitated.*)

ROBERT. (*An outburst.*) Goddamit, I want it on my terms, I don't wanna be politely bounced! I want control, I feel like I'm losing control of my life and I just can't fucking stand it!!! (*Pause. Robert is as surprised about the outburst as Catherine.*) Jesus. (*Takes a long swig of wine.*)

CATHERINE. That was terrific, Robert. If this were group we'd all be giving you a standing ovation.
ROBERT. What?
CATHERINE. Want some more wine?
ROBERT. Yes. (*Catherine pours more wine in both cups; Robert watches her disapprovingly.*) Doesn't the wine . . . conflict with the Thorazine?
CATHERINE. Complement. Yin and yang.
ROBERT. I wish you wouldn't.
CATHERINE. Rob— (*Robert reaches for the bottle.*) Robert! (*Pulls the bottle away from him, spills wine from her cup.*) I don't need that shit, not at all. (*Tries to change the mood.*) Besides, I'm celebrating, too. (*Pause. She repeats herself, louder.*) I'm celebrating, too.
ROBERT. Oh? (*Catherine goes to her desk, gets a sheaf of poems, gives them to Robert.*) Oh. When did you—?
CATHERINE. Recently.
ROBERT. Really? Oh.
CATHERINE. Those copies are for you. I can autograph 'em, if you want. (*Pause: Robert reads.*) Still pretty rough. Not finished. I haven't gotten my stride back. Football player doesn't jump right into the world series his first day out, right?
ROBERT. Right. Gotta run a few laps first.
CATHERINE. Right.
ROBERT. (*Reading.*) Hm.
CATHERINE. What.
ROBERT. What?
CATHERINE. Why the "hm"?
ROBERT. I like it.
CATHERINE. Which one'd you read, lemme see. (*Takes the poem.*) Oh, well, it's the writing that counts, not the product. Who cares if it's bad.
ROBERT. I liked it.
CATHERINE. It's the process that counts. Diving in, deeper and deeper, as fast as you can move the pen, not knowing

when you'll come up.

ROBERT. Or if you'll come up?

CATHERINE. Yeah, well, there's always that sense of danger.

ROBERT. Danger?

CATHERINE. Yeah. You know that. (*Robert looks at her.*) Well, read. (*Takes the next poem away.*) Not that one, no. (*Robert puts them back in the envelope.*) Robert.

ROBERT. I'll read 'em later. I'll take 'em to the office.

CATHERINE. Don't get caught.

ROBERT. Was that an insult?

CATHERINE. No! Jesus, don't be so paranoid. (*Beat, then she laughs.*)

ROBERT. Don't laugh at me!

CATHERINE. What?

ROBERT. You sit up here with your pills and your weird music, looking down your nose at the whole world. That job is my life! (*Pause. Catherine turns away, hurt.*) Shit. Maybe I should come in again, and start over. (*Robert goes to her, embraces her, then kisses her.*) Oh. I wanna make love, I been thinking about making love with you since— (*Tries to kiss her, but Catherine gently but firmly pulls away.*) What's—?

CATHERINE. I really don't care to be just a stockbroker's sexual daydream. The wine, the poet's garret, the poet.

ROBERT. Can you please stop being so nasty to me!?! (*A pause. Then Robert stands, starts to put on his coat.*) I gotta go for a walk.

CATHERINE. I'm sorry about your job, Robert.

ROBERT. It's just a job, I can get another one, no problem, I can take my pick. And I think you're drinking too much, end of patronizing advice. (*Robert goes to the door.*) We'll eat our celebratory dinner another time.

CATHERINE. Tomorrow?

ROBERT. Well, no, not tomorrow, I've got a business dinner. (*Laughs.*) With the chairman.

CATHERINE. (*Gives Robert the poems.*) Don't forget these.
ROBERT. (*Takes them.*) Oh.
CATHERINE. Robert.
ROBERT. Yes?
CATHERINE. Bye. (*Robert hesitates, then exits. Catherine sits quietly for a long moment.*) Oh shit. (*A light fades up on Joanne.*)
JOANNE. Did you oversleep?
CATHERINE. (*Distracted.*) What?
JOANNE. You're late, Catherine.
CATHERINE. Oh. No, I was working.
JOANNE. With Alice?
CATHERINE. Writing.
JOANNE. I see. (*Catherine crosses to Joanne's area, sits.*) How's it going?
CATHERINE. All right.
JOANNE. Good.
CATHERINE. No, it's not. It's all surface. It comes fast but I can't get a grasp on it. I can't make it mean anything, I can't make it good.
JOANNE. It has to be good? (*Catherine looks at Joanne, surprised, then laughs.*) Do you really expect your work to be at the old level, so soon?
CATHERINE. No, I guess not, since I've changed so much. The schizophrenia's turned me into a sexy woman and a bad poet.
JOANNE. Why do you say that?
CATHERINE. Wanna read my new stuff?
JOANNE. Yes, if you'd like me to.
CATHERINE. Roses are red
Violets are blue
I'm a schizophrenic
And so am I (*Long pause. Joanne starts writing in her notes.*)
JOANNE. Sleeping all right?
CATHERINE. No.

JOANNE. Symptoms? Catherine?
CATHERINE. Nothing I can't . . . ignore.
JOANNE. Voices? Catherine, are you hearing any . . . ?
CATHERINE. I feel like I'm on trial.
JOANNE. I'm sorry you feel that way.
CATHERINE. I'm all right. (*Catherine shrugs.*)
JOANNE. I think we should increase the Thorazine to— (*Consulting her notes.*) —three hundred and fifty—
CATHERINE. No.
JOANNE. Pardon?
CATHERINE. I can't increase the Thorazine.
JOANNE. And why not?
CATHERINE. A writer writes. It's bad, it's awful, but at some point it will be brilliant, soon enough. (*Pauses, then suddenly:*) Without the poetry, the schizophrenia's all I have!
JOANNE. Oh, Catherine.
CATHERINE. Increase the vitamins. (*A beat.*) No. Write it down. No. No! (*Catherine stands, crosses to the apartment. Puts on record. She picks up a poem reads:*) The sweet wine I drank
From your lovely young mouth
The wine of your kiss
The hot sun of your . . . (*Laughs.*) Oh God . . . (*Alice enters.*) I want it back, want it back, want it back. . . . (*Alice knocks at the door.*) What? Oh, Alice. (*Alice enters the apartment.*)
ALICE. I thought I'd stop by.
CATHERINE. Oh, yeah.
ALICE. How you doing?
CATHERINE. Did I . . . ?
ALICE. Hm?
CATHERINE. Was I supposed to . . . ?
ALICE. (*Pauses, looks at her.*) Monday. Ten A.M. (*Alice looks around a bit, finally starts listening to the music.*) God. (*Goes to the stereo, rejects the record.*) What is this, the soundtrack to a Jackson Pollock painting? (*Beat.*) Writing,

eh? You supposed to drink wine on top of all those bizarr chemicals?

CATHERINE. Want some?

ALICE. (*Picks up the bottle, looks at the label.*) Jesus.

CATHERINE. A present.

ALICE. How is Robert, anyway?

CATHERINE. (*Gives her some wine.*) Who? Here.

ALICE. I'm interrupting you, you're busy.

CATHERINE. It's okay.

ALICE. You're looking extremely beautiful. (*Beat.*) I read your poems, they're not very good. Sit down, will you?

CATHERINE. No.

ALICE. Of course, you know that, right?

CATHERINE. You angry at me?

ALICE. No, anybody can write bad poetry, it's no reason to get angry. This is really good wine, how much did it cost?

CATHERINE. It's free.

ALICE. Read the Stein book yet?

CATHERINE. No, not yet, Jesus, Alice.

ALICE. Better get going, meeting's on Monday.

CATHERINE. That all you care about?

ALICE. No, I care about you guzzling fifty dollar wine and writing shit, absolute garbage. Thorazine poetry. Who do you think you're kidding?! (*Slams the poems down on the table, angrily, immediately regrets it, covers her face.*) Oh, babe, I'm . . . (*Pauses.*) Why does anybody take me seriously? Sometimes I wanna say to everyone "It's all been a horrible mistake, I'm sorry, everybody go home."

CATHERINE. A little while ago, all I heard from you was "Write. Work on the book. Write."

ALICE. Don't hold me liable for my bullshit, you oughta know better than that. I'm not gonna take responsibility for your sanity, or your work. (*Catherine angrily takes poems from the table, tosses them into the wastebasket.*) Don't lay that guilt shit one me, I don't care if you're crazy, I won't put up with it! (*A pause. Catherine turns away. Alice pours herself more wine.*) You want my opinion? Marry Robert. He loves you and that's a rare and precious thing these days, God knows. Settle down to a life of . . . good wine and fine music on the twenty eighth floor. Be . . . sensible. Stay away from fucked up manipulative type A's like me.

CATHERINE. You're afraid of me, aren't you. I can feel you pulling away.

ALICE. You do sort of basically scare me shitless. It's why I love you. I gotta get outa here. (*Puts on her coat, crosses to the door, stops. She turns, goes to Catherine's desk, gets the Stein ms. Alice exits. After a moment, Catherine starts the stereo again. Music: more Crumb.* A spot fades up on Robert. Catherine hesitates, then dials her phone. A phone rings once.*)

ROBERT. Hello.

CATHERINE. Robert.

ROBERT. Catherine, that you?

CATHERINE. C'est moi. How are you?

ROBERT. I'm . . . okay. You?

CATHERINE. You busy?

ROBERT. Well, I'm working, yeah.

CATHERINE. No time to talk?

ROBERT. No, no. I mean, yeah, I do. I'm just a bit preoccupied.

CATHERINE. Where you been? I haven't heard from you.

ROBERT. I've been busy.

CATHERINE. Quit yet?

ROBERT. (*After a slight pause.*) Today, yeah. In fact, I gave the letter of resignation to the chairman's secretary about fifteen minutes ago.

CATHERINE. Wanna go to a movie?

ROBERT. A movie? (*Laughs politely.*) Oh. . . .

CATHERINE. Robert, I wanna see you. It's been more than a week now. I know this is a rough time for you with your

*See Special Note on copyright page.

job, but you know it's really terrible to drink that fine wine alone, I really miss—

ROBERT. (*Cuts in, nervously.*) Catherine, can you hold a minute, just a minute? (*Pause. Robert steps back, takes a deep breath, releases it. Catherine is very still.*) Sorry. A client just—

CATHERINE. Can we meet at the park? It's important.

ROBERT. I'll take an early lunch. (*Catherine hangs up. Robert steps into the bare stage area, pacing nervously in the cold wind, hands in pockets. Catherine, after a moment, puts on a coat, joins Robert.*)

CATHERINE. Robert.

ROBERT. (*Startled, turns.*) Oh.

CATHERINE. Scare you?

ROBERT. No, no. I'm just cold. It didn't occur to me to bring my thermals when I—

CATHERINE. I like the park.

ROBERT. I've only got time for coffee. Let's go over to—

CATHERINE. Let's stay here, it's nice.

ROBERT. Nice?

CATHERINE. The wind is clean.

ROBERT. The wind is cold.

CATHERINE. That's what I mean.

ROBERT. (*Looks at her, a beat.*) I know you detest the question, but what the hell: are you okay?

CATHERINE. C'mere.

ROBERT. What?

CATHERINE. Come here. (*Pause. Robert goes to her, reluctantly. Catherine takes his head in her hands, looks intently into his eyes.*)

ROBERT. Your hands're cold.

CATHERINE. I wanted to see the soft blue suns behind your eyes.

ROBERT. You said it was important.

CATHERINE. It is.

ROBERT. (*Slight pause.*) You've been drinking.

CATHERINE. Rich warm red wine. (*Catherine kisses him gently.*)
ROBERT. You shouldn't be drinking on top of your medication. God, I'm sorry I bought you that wine.
CATHERINE. San Francisco?
ROBERT. What?
CATHERINE. Going to San Francisco?
ROBERT. I wouldn't think so. I'll be sending my resume around, as soon as it comes back from the printers. Cath—
CATHERINE. Gonna take up watercolors?
ROBERT. Catherine. What was so important?
CATHERINE. I wanted to . . . see you.
ROBERT. You called me away from the office just because you wanted to—
CATHERINE. It's been a week and a half.
ROBERT. (*Sharply.*) It hasn't been— (*Stops himself, looks around self-consciously.*) Well, it hasn't been a week and a half.
CATHERINE. I've been writing.
ROBERT. Good.
CATHERINE. And I wanted to find out what you thought of my new poems. I mean, I think . . . it's pretty important. (*Pause. Then Robert takes the envelope of poems out of his coat pocket.*)
ROBERT. I haven't read them yet. I've been pretty— (*Catherine suddenly giggles.*) What?
CATHERINE. You look good in gooseflesh.
ROBERT. (*Slight pause.*) Well, I've been, as you can imagine, pretty preoccupied. I'll give them back. Here. (*Holds out the envelope.*)
CATHERINE. This is incredible!
ROBERT. What?
CATHERINE. (*Laughing.*) I feel like I'm in the middle of some crazy magnetic field, everybody's bouncing off, I'm fucking impregnable!
ROBERT. It's just that this is a bad time for me.

CATHERINE. There's something going around.
ROBERT. (*Laughs nervously.*) Yeah. Look, I gotta find another job, I just don't know any other way to live, it's all I can think about. And I think it would be better if we didn't see each other, not for a—
CATHERINE. (*Takes a step backward.*) Yeah.
ROBERT. Not for a while. I'm worried about you, Catherine, and . . .
CATHERINE. Yeah?
ROBERT. And I think it might be better if I . . . stayed away from you. (*Catherine is laughing.*) Fuck. Catherine? Do you understand what I'm . . . trying to say?
CATHERINE. I opened the last bottle.
ROBERT. Jesus, I wish you wouldn't—
CATHERINE. It's breathing now, it's waiting for us, it's very important.
ROBERT. What're you suggesting, that we go drink wine? That's—
CATHERINE. (*Shouts.*) I love you!!!
ROBERT. Dammit, there are people looking at us, how dare you embarrass me like— (*Takes a beat, looks around self-consciously.*) You have a real skill, you know that? You can provoke me. I thought I divorced the only person who could do that. You're not taking your medication, are you?
CATHERINE. I'm writing.
ROBERT. Shit.
CATHERINE. God, how I want it, the power, the thunderstorms, scraming purple skies, clouds squealing crazy wonderful music, can you hear it? The sun, the stars, the seaside bars, and all the cars, going to Mars. (*Laughs.*) I'm working with rhyme now. Are you cold, Robert? Are you cold? C'mere. (*Embraces him hungrily.*) God, I wanna taste you, taste something rich and buttery like your wine, red wine that spurts out—
ROBERT. Catherine. (*Holds her hands, tightly.*) Catherine, Jesus, stop it. Stop it. Don't you know where we are? (*Beat:*

he looks around again.) What's happening to you?

CATHERINE. I'm writing. Writers write. I love you. That's a quote. Do you love me? Listen. The sun the moon, and the darkness at noon, you'll leave again soon, I cry and I croon.

ROBERT. Catherine.

CATHERINE. Listen to the music. You'll like the music, the music is beautiful. Do you hear it? Can you hear it?

ROBERT. (*After a pause.*) Yes. (*Catherine looks at him for a moment, then laughs, then moves away.*)

CATHERINE. Yeah?

ROBERT. (*Goes to her, gently, carefully.*) C'mon, let's go . . . home. I'll take you home, okay? We'll make a quick phone call, then get a cab. We'll call Alice.

CATHERINE. I'm okay.

ROBERT. C'mon. (*Pulls gently.*)

CATHERINE. (*Firmly.*) No. I wanna stay here.

ROBERT. Please.

CATHERINE. No, I'm fine. (*Robert hesitates, then takes off his coat, wraps it around Catherine's shoulders.*)

ROBERT. Here. I'm gonna make a quick call, then I just wanna . . . let the office know where I am, then I'll be right back. Okay? Catherine?

CATHERINE. Yeah.

ROBERT. You'll be okay?

CATHERINE. Yeah, sure. (*Robert hesitates, then exits. A moment: Catherine alone. Lights fade to blackout. Loud music: Peter Maxwell Davies' "8 Songs for a Mad King,"* crashingly crazy, piercing music. Pounding on a door. In darkness:*)

ROBERT. Catherine!

CATHERINE. No.

ROBERT. Catherine, are you in there?

CATHERINE. Nooooo. . . .

ROBERT. (*More pounding.*) Catherine!?

CATHERINE. (*Screams.*) Go away! (*Lights up: Catherine is*

*See Special Note on copyright page.

in her very messy apartment, a blanket wrapped around her.)

ROBERT. Catherine, it's Robert. Lemme in.

CATHERINE. I'm busy.

ROBERT. C'mon, I know better than that.

CATHERINE. No! Go away, I can't hear you, I'm not going to listen to you—

ROBERT. Catherine, we're real! Open the door. If you don't—

CATHERINE. No!

ROBERT. —we'll call the police, now— (*Loud pounding.*) —open the goddam door!!! (*Pounding continues. Catherine scrambles to her feet, crosses quickly to the door, unlocks it, goes back to her spot on the floor, wraps herself with the blanket. A moment, then the door opens and Robert enters, looking around. Alice enters, stands by the door.*)

CATHERINE. Robert. Hello.

ROBERT. God.

CATHERINE. Guess what. Life has focus.

ROBERT. Are you . . . ?

CATHERINE. Oh, I'm fine, maybe a little too much California sunshine.

ROBERT. (*Touches her.*) You're shaking.

CATHERINE. Maybe I'm not, maybe you're the one that's shaking. (*Alice laughs.*)

ROBERT. (*Sharply.*) I don't wanna hear that shit, Alice.

ALICE. Fuck off, Robert.

ROBERT. Can't you see what she's—?

ALICE. I can see and I've seen it before. I told you—

ROBERT. Just don't make it—

ALICE. Robert, get off my—

ROBERT. (*Overlapping.*) Just don't— (*Catherine screams. It starts low but builds quickly and frighteningly and continues long after Robert and Alice have stopped bickering and stare at her in horror.*) Catherine. (*Embraces her; she tries to pull away, but he holds her. Alice turns away.*) Catherine. Catherine.

ALICE. Jesus. It's freezing in here. (*Pause. Catherine finally relaxes.*)
CATHERINE. Robert.
ROBERT. Yeah.
CATHERINE. I wrote a poem for you. Listen. The time I tried. To stand by your side. And although I cried. (*Alice is looking through the papers on the writing desk.*) I smiled and I lied. Because of my— (*To Alice.*) Don't! They're in rough shape.
ALICE. And so are you, babe. You're relapsing.
CATHERINE. Life has focus.
ALICE. Lucky you. (*Alice lights a cigarette. Robert turns off the stereo.*)
ROBERT. There's pills all over the floor.
CATHERINE. It's over.
ROBERT. What's over?
CATHERINE. It.
ROBERT. What!?
CATHERINE. What?
ALICE. Robert, give it up. Jesus.
ROBERT. (*Pauses, calmer.*) You've seen her like this before?
ALICE. Twice.
ROBERT. Which hospital?
ALICE. Mercy General. I'll . . . drop you off but I won't go in. I can't take any of this, Robert, I just wanna. . . .
ROBERT. Why don't you wait in the car. (*Alice hesitates briefly, looking at Catherine, then exits.*) Catherine. Come on. Let's go. Catherine.
CATHERINE. Are you going to San Francisco?
ROBERT. (*Slight pause.*) No.
CATHERINE. Are we going to celebrate?
ROBERT. (*Firmly.*) Catherine. Let's go.
CATHERINE. I couldn't have done it without you. .Thank you.
ROBERT. Catherine, let's—
CATHERINE. I wrote a poem for you. (*Catherine puts her*

hands on Robert's face. Robert tenses. Catherine kisses him gently.) Robert. (*A beat. Then Robert embraces Catherine, passionately. Joanne enters the bare stage area opposite.*)

JOANNE. Robert.

ROBERT. (*Startled.*) What?

JOANNE. Robert?

ROBERT. Yes.

JOANNE. My name is Joanne. I'm a friend of Catherine's. (*Robert and Catherine leave the apartment, joining Joanne.*) Catherine? Catherine, can you hear me?

ROBERT. I don't think she's been taking her . . . medicine. (*Laughs; it catches in her throat.*)

JOANNE. Robert, why don't you have a seat in the waiting area and I'll speak with you in a moment.

ROBERT. All right. (*Looks at Catherine for a brief moment, then exits. Joanne takes a small flashlight, snaps it on, passes it in front of Catherine's eyes. Catherine reacts.*)

CATHERINE. What?

JOANNE. Catherine.

CATHERINE. Yes.

JOANNE. Do you know where you are?

CATHERINE. Yes.

JOANNE. Good. (*Looks at her for a moment.*) I don't think it's going to be as bad this time.

CATHERINE. Where's Robert?

JOANNE. He's here. (*Another beat.*) I'm going to go make the arrangements, upstairs, okay? (*Touches Catherine's face.*) How are you feeling?

CATHERINE. I'll be all right.

JOANNE. I know. (*Turns, exits. Tableau: Catherine alone.*)

CATHERINE. I'll be all right. (*A moment, then the lights fade to blackout.*)

CURTAIN

PROPERTY PLOT

SET PROPS

In Catherine's apartment:

kitchen table (approx 2'x3')
wastebaskets (by desk and sink)
small writing desk
platform bed with mattress (mattress must come off)
sheets
blankets
two pillows
bedspread
large floor pillows (fit under the bed)
desk chair
two kitchen table chairs
kitchen sink (no water needed but it must drain)
about 8 milk crates for shelves
clothes in crates
books in crates
record albums in crates
framed poster (music concert)
rug
jar of pencils (on desk)
stereo system (expensive looking and practical)
floorlamp, gooseneck (practical, by bed)
desk lamp (practical)

yellow pads of paper (on desk)
telephone
pitcher of water
alarm clock
water glasses
ceramic coffee cups
pill bottles (vitamins, one large
prescription bottle, practical)
tray for pills
dishrag (to cover pill tray)
corkscrew
slim hardcover books (2)
sheaf of poems (10 pages, typed)
manila envelopes

In the psychiatrist's office:

small desk
swivel chair (behind desk)
office chair
yellow notepad
pen
photo (framed)
medical files

In the lunch scene
(can be preset or taken on in a blackout):

small round restaurant table
two chairs
bottle of German wine
two wineglasses
ashtray

In Alice's office (Act Two):

office waiting room chair (can be brought on in black)
magazine

In the hospital (Act two):

Chair (brought on in black)

PERSONAL PROPS

Catherine:

currency (in pocket of coat, for lunch scene)

Robert:

plastic wine glass (party scene)
currency (party scene, in pocket)
pen (in pocket)
2 bottles of wine in paper bags
wine in a bottle (should be cleanable from his shirt)
wooden case of red wine
two crystal wineglasses in cardboard box
sheaf of poems (pocket of coat)

Joanne:

poetry books (same as in Catherine's apartment)
medical ID (final scene)
stethoscope (final scene)
small medical flashlight (in pocket, final scene)

Alice:

cigarettes
book length manuscript in cardboard box
cigarette lighter (final scene)

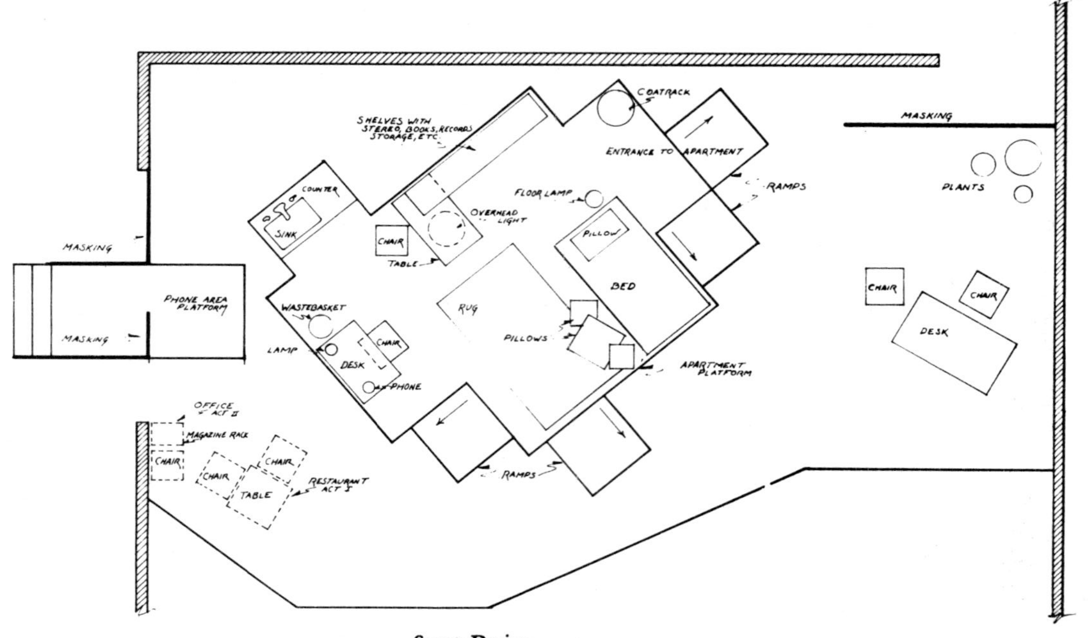

—Scene Design—

"STANDING ON MY KNEES"

(Designed by John J. Murbach
for the Wisdom Bridge Theatre)

New PLAYS

EASTERN STANDARD
BORDERLINES
AMULETS AGAINST THE DRAGON FORCES
THE MAGIC ACT
KILLERS
THE DEATH OF PAPA
IMPASSIONED EMBRACES
CLEVER DICK
LOVE MINUS
BIG MARY
FAITH, HOPE & CHARITY
ELECTION YEAR & SO WHEN WE GET MARRIED
TWO EGGS SCRAMBLED SOFT & A BRIEF PERIOD OF TIME